How Embarrassing Is That?

by

Pete Johnson

First published in 2007 in Great Britain by
Barrington Stoke Ltd
18 Walker St, Edinburgh EH3 7LP

www.barringtonstoke.co.uk

Reprinted 2007

ISBN: 978-1-84299-450-4

Printed in Great Britain by Bell & Bain Ltd

A Note from the Author

It was the worst moment of my whole life.

I was thirteen. And I was at a mate's party. I was looking really cool. Even girls noticed me. It was brilliant. And then I saw something terrible. My parents had walked into the party.

Could my night get any worse? Yes, it could. For then my parents started yelling out my name. They said they'd tried ringing on the doorbell first, but no one had heard them. But that was no excuse for their terrible behaviour, was it? I thought I'd die of shame. I didn't ... But my parents went on doing terrible things. At home, when my friends came round, my parents didn't just hand out food and drinks and go away. No, they actually started talking to *my* friends – sometimes for over a minute.

And if ever I met my mum and dad in town they wouldn't just mutter, '*Hello*' softly and rush away. No, they would walk along beside me so everyone could see. Shameless – or what?

And now, after talking to some teenagers, I've found out that parents are behaving just as badly today. In fact, I heard some incredible stories. So that's what this book is all about – very embarrassing parents. It's a horror story really. But I hope it will make you laugh too.

And the ending might shock you. But I shan't say any more now. See you over the page.

Contents

Chapter 1

The Worst Moment Of My Life

"Hi, Tiddles!"

The words blasted out across the playground. My blood froze with horror, and Grace, my best friend, said, "What scary parents. And who is Tiddles? Their cat?"

She laughed and I tried to laugh too. But it's hard to laugh when terror has taken a grip of you.

It was an open day at my school. Parents could walk around the school and in on any lesson they wanted. All the other parents were just looking around without any fuss. Only two were making a right show of themselves – *mine*.

Ever since I'd come to this school I'd done my best to hide my mum and dad away. It wasn't very hard, actually. You see, we live four miles away from the school. I just made sure I never had any friends round to my house.

And I'd torn up the letter about the open day as well. So I really thought I was safe. But somehow my parents must have found out about it.

"Tiddles, over here!" They were waving at me now as well. It was break time, so just about the whole school was watching them. I could feel an enormous blush break out across my face.

Grace was staring at them ... and then at me. "They seem to be calling to you," she said, in a shocked voice. "Do you know them, Ruby?"

"Never seen them before," I said at once. Then I added, "Well, I do know them a tiny little bit ... they're my mum and dad, actually."

Callum, my other best friend, rushed up. "Embarrassing parent alert!" he cried. "Who do you think Tiddles is?"

"I'm afraid I'm Tiddles," I whispered.

Then my parents bounced over to us. They had huge grins all over their faces. "Hi, gang!" screeched Mum. Then she added with a happy grin, "And hello, Tiddles!"

So why do they call me Tiddles?

Well, when I was about three, I wet myself – and the story is I cried out, "I've done tiddles in my pants." My parents laughed for about a year and even now, when I'm almost thirteen, they still go on calling me Tiddles. (Sometimes they call me Miss Tiddles, which I think is even worse.)

"But doesn't your school look great?" cried Mum. She and Dad get excited at just about everything. It's very, very tiring. My bad luck – this week they were both on holiday. Dad wears suits to go to work – he does something very boring in a bank. So when he gets a day off he goes mad. Like today. It was only March but Dad was already in his summer shorts and sandals. As for Mum's top … well, it was far too tight on her, for a start.

"You forgot to tell us about the parents' day," said Dad to me. "Bad girl. It was just lucky I saw another parent on their way here … Still, I know you have a lot on your mind. Ruby works ever so hard," he said, in the loudest whisper you've ever heard. "She spends hours and hours on her homework. We have to keep telling her to chill out."

My face felt so red now, I thought it might even burst. Grace gave my hand a little squeeze. She knew I was suffering.

But then Mum turned to my friends and cried, "Now don't tell me your names – you're Grace."

"That's right," she answered.

"I was so sorry to hear about that boy dumping you," went on Mum.

I gasped. Grace stared back at Mum with her mouth wide open.

"Oh, yes, I know all about that," said Mum.

Oh, no, you don't, I wanted to yell. *I didn't tell you. You just heard me talking to Grace on the phone one day.*

"And you must be Callum," said Mum. "And I don't think you're short at all.

Anyway, being small hasn't done Tom Cruise any harm, has it?"

I couldn't even look at Callum. The thing he worried about most was how short he was. And Mum had just put her big foot right in it.

"You see," said Mum, "Ruby and I don't have any secrets ... we're more like friends really. We have a very open relationship. Ruby knows she can tell us anything – we won't be shocked. So you can just chat away to us. We even listen to the same music as you. We're always down-loading new stuff off the internet."

She thought we'd be glad about that. But who wants their parents to like the same music as them?

Then Dad started talking. He had this little smile on his face. I groaned.

"Now, here's a question for you bright young people ... What's the world's longest word? Anyone know?" Before we could answer he said, "Smile – because there's a mile in it!" Dad chuckled away to himself, with Mum joining in.

"Now," he went on, "who can tell me what the fastest part of a car is? The *dash*board, of course!" On and on Dad went, telling one terrible joke after another. (He gets them off the internet.)

He didn't seem to notice the fake little laughs which Grace and Callum were forcing out after all of his jokes.

At last, the bell rang. I'd never been so happy for break to finish.

"Well, we'd better go," I said quickly. "Can't be late for Miss Wells."

"But we're coming with you," said Mum. Even she must have noticed the horrified look on my face, because she patted my head – right in front of everyone. Then she said,

"Now, don't look so worried, Ruby. We'll sit at the back and we won't make a sound."

I whispered to Callum and Grace that they could go now. They'd been so brave. They'd put up with my parents all through break. I couldn't ask any more – not even from my best friends. So they sped away while Mum called after them, "So lovely to have met you both at last!"

Then I walked over to the English block. My legs were trembling. Mum and Dad were on each side of me, chattering away like two excited monkeys.

"I suppose we'd better tell your English teacher we're dropping in," said Dad.

Now, my teacher, Miss Wells, is very strict. And I really didn't think she'd like Mum and Dad in the lesson. She might even tell them they couldn't stay. That would be great. "Yes," I said, "I think it's a good idea to see Miss Wells."

She wasn't in the classroom but I thought she might be in the stockroom next door. The door was half-open. I watched Mum and Dad knock and walk in.

I heard Dad call out. "Miss Wells," he shouted, "you've got two keen new pupils." He went on sadly, "Ah, no one in here, but what a lot of books." Then he let out a yell like an excited three-year-old. "Oh, look, here's *The War of the Worlds*! I remember reading that at school. Marvellous book."

All at once I had an idea.

The stockroom door was kept open, because it stuck if anyone closed it. What if someone suddenly closed it now? My mum and dad would be trapped inside – and I'd have peace at last!

So, I checked no one was watching, then I rushed forward and slammed the door shut. My heart was thumping like mad and I dashed into the classroom.

"Where are your mum and dad?" asked Callum.

"Oh, they had to go," I said quickly, and sat down.

Chapter 2
Locking Up My Parents

Miss Wells swept into the classroom. Everyone shut up at once. She could be very bad-tempered. She once gave a boy a detention because he was breathing too loudly.

She started talking about homework. Then I jumped. I could hear a noise like a far-away rumble of thunder. It had to be my parents banging at the stockroom door trying to get out.

Locking your mum and dad in a stockroom
– that's bad, isn't it? I knew I should get
them out now. But then I thought about what
they'd do in the classroom. They'd talk very
loudly and laugh at their own terrible jokes –
and ruin my life. So it was their fault really.
They'd driven me to it.

And anyway, I wasn't going to keep them
in there all day. As soon as English was over
I'd get them out. There were masses of books
to read in the stockroom, so they had
something to do.

Then I heard that thumping noise again.
This was awful. But no one else seemed to
hear my parents – only me. Maybe I was
feeling so guilty I just *thought* I heard
thumping. Yes, that must be it.

Then there was silence. Peace at last.
Unless ... unless there wasn't enough air in
that stockroom. And at this moment both my
parents were gasping for breath!

I stood up fast and asked if I could go to the toilet. Miss Wells was cross. She hissed at me to hurry up. I sped down the corridor. I thought I'd listen in at the door of the stockroom, just to check I could hear breathing. If I could, I'd leave my parents there until the end of English.

I put my ear right up to the door and tried to listen. Then I saw someone was watching me.

The caretaker was a big, sweaty man, who was always lurking somewhere around. And right now he was looking at me in a very puzzled way.

"Oh, hello," I said. Then I tried to sound friendly. I added, "It's very warm for March, isn't it?"

But he just grunted, "What exactly are you doing?"

"Er, well, my mum and dad were supposed to be in English, but they've vanished."

Suddenly, from inside the stockroom came loud shrieking from both my parents.

The caretaker blinked in shock, then he took a massive bunch of keys out of his pocket. After a bit of pushing he got the door open. Mum and Dad fell out.

"Oh, well done," cried Mum.

"But how on earth did you get stuck in there?" the caretaker asked.

"I expect someone closed that door for a little joke. Still, no harm done," said Dad, as cheerful as ever. "And we knew our daughter would come to our rescue ... in the end."

It would never have entered Mum or Dad's heads that I was the one who'd locked them in.

Miss Wells frowned at me when I went back into the classroom. "Where have you been?" she began. Then she saw my parents grinning madly at her.

"Sorry we're late," said Dad, "but we got stuck in your stockroom. Now, we'll just sit very still somewhere." He added, with a merry smile, "When I was at school I was known as teacher's pet. I was kept in a cage at the back of the room!"

Then, chuckling away, they sat down. They made a lot of noise. Miss Wells watched them in stunned silence.

Callum whispered to me, "You locked your parents in that stockroom, didn't you?"

I nodded.

"And I'd have done exactly the same," he said.

Chapter 3
The Ouch Factor

It was half past three. And the longest day of my whole life was over at last.

Callum only lived four doors away from the school. As well as his bedroom, he had his own little room downstairs. It was called his den. His dad and step-mum never bothered him in there. Neither did his two younger sisters. It was totally private – totally brilliant.

Grace, Callum and I always chatted and laughed when we were on our own together. Today, I didn't say a word. You can't when you're still in a state of shock. After a long time I moaned in a low voice, "I'll never get over today, will I?"

"Yes, you will," said Callum firmly. "Your parents weren't that bad."

I looked up.

"Well, all right, they were," he admitted.

"Just answer this," I said. "At lunchtime, did my mum really sniff the air and start singing *Food, Glorious Food?*"

Callum and Grace looked at each other. "I'm afraid she did," said Grace softly.

"I just thought I might have dreamt that bit."

17

"Not everyone heard them," said Grace brightly. "Her singing voice wasn't that loud."

Then I asked, "And when they left, did they both kiss me?"

"The biggest, sloppiest kisses I've ever seen," said Callum.

Grace gave him a stern look.

"She had to know," murmured Callum.

I put my hands over my eyes. "I'll never live this down, will I?"

Callum and Grace said nothing.

"My life's over, isn't it?" I said.

"Oh, no," cried Grace. "I'm sure people will forget ... in time."

"Do you know the really awful thing?" I said. "My mum and dad will think they were a big success and everyone thought they were fantastic. They won't have a clue what they've done." I shook my head. "I tried so hard to keep them a secret. It's no fun having the most embarrassing parents ever."

"You're wrong there," cut in Grace suddenly.

"You mean you've found parents who are more embarrassing than mine?" I cried.

"Mine," said Grace.

We both stared at her.

"I also destroyed that open-day letter," she said. "Because no one must ever meet my parents. Have you ever thought about why I never invite you round to my house?"

"I just thought that was because Callum's house was so near," I said. "But your parents can't be as bad as mine."

"They're even worse," she said.

"That's impossible!" I cried. "No other parents sing *Food, Glorious Food* in front of the whole school, or tell the most awful jokes ..."

"My dad never tells jokes!" cried Grace. "In fact, he only smiles about twice a year. And he talks to you as if you're three years old."

Callum was looking at us both. He had a gleam in his eye. "You know, this is a very interesting problem – whose parents are the most embarrassing. We ought to find out." He grinned. "You've heard of the X-Factor. This will be the *Ouch* Factor. We'll spend some time with your parents first, Grace. Your dad sounds so awful, I can't wait to meet him. And then yours, Ruby. We'll award marks for everything embarrassing they do. Then we'll add up the scores and see who the winner is. What do you think?"

Grace said slowly, "Well, I know my parents will easily win."

I shook my head. "I'm sorry, but no parents are more terrible than mine."

"It should be a great competition," Callum said.

We made up a list of embarrassing things. Then we worked out a score list.

One point if a parent wore clothes that were too young for them, or had a loud voice or an annoying laugh.

Two points if they tried to talk about bands today or used hip words.

Three points if they were fussy about things that don't matter, or talked about schoolwork with your mates.

Four points if they made a show of you in any way, such as helping you cross the road, or telling you off in front of your mates.

Five points for singing or dancing in public.

Six points (maximum) for giving you a big kiss or hug anywhere, anytime.

"We may think of some other things later," said Callum. "But that gives you an idea of how the scoring will work." Then he added, "As I haven't got a parent in the competition, I'll be the judge."

Grace and I agreed this was fair.

Then Grace said, "But are you really sure you want to meet my dad? Why don't we just go to the Chamber of Horrors instead."

"No, I can't wait for this competition to start," said Callum. "And may the worst parents win."

Chapter 4

A High-Scoring Evening

Two days later Callum and I went round to Grace's house.

She whispered at the door, "You are coming into my house at your own risk. Whatever happens ... well, you asked for it."

Then her mum came to the door. She smiled and said, "I'm so happy to meet you both," in a normal sort of way.

We put our school bags down, and then she asked us, ever so politely, if we'd mind taking our shoes off. This was something we never had to do at Callum's house.

"There you are, that's five points right away," whispered Grace.

"Oh, no," Callum said, "your mum didn't make a big deal about it. She only scores one point for that."

We tip-toed into the sitting room.

The house smelt very clean – and everything sparkled and shone. "Is it always as tidy as this?" I asked Grace.

"Oh, yes," she answered grimly. "I have to help clean at the weekends as well. What fun."

"Well, so far, your parents have only scored one point," said Callum.

"You wait," Grace said. "You just wait."

A few moments later Grace's mum came into the sitting room. She asked in a very soft voice, "Would you all just follow me, please?"

The three of us went after her to the front door. She shook her head as if something really bad had happened. "There was very nearly a serious accident here," she said, and she pointed to where we'd flung our bags down in the hallway. "Never, ever leave bags out like that – most of all at night." Her voice got a fraction louder. "Put them somewhere safe now, please," she said.

We put them in a little cupboard under the stairs.

"Yes, they'll be out of danger there," Grace's mum agreed.

I suddenly giggled. I couldn't help it. She was talking about our bags as if they were bombs about to explode.

A bit later Grace's mum came in with a tray of drinks and biscuits. We dived on to it. Then we heard murmurings in the hallway. "Dad's back," muttered Grace.

The door opened and Grace's dad walked in. He was a big man with a very red face. He had slippers on and they made a loud, flapping noise every time he moved. I wanted to laugh.

"Good evening, children," he said, as if we were about six. "Grace's friends are always welcome." Then he said more loudly, "Grace, have you asked your guests if they'd like anything else to eat? I see their plates are all empty."

Grace started to go red. "No, I haven't," she mumbled. Then she asked Callum and me, "Would you like any more food?"

Callum and I both said quickly that we didn't want any.

"They're just being polite," snapped her dad. "Bring some more food in. I shouldn't have to tell you to look after your guests."

Grace got up quickly and went out. Then her dad turned to Callum. "Do you find Maths as difficult as Grace does?" he asked.

"Well, yes, I suppose so," began Callum. "I hate fractions."

"Fractions are easy," cried her dad, "if you put your mind to it."

Then he turned to me. "What's your best subject, Ruby?"

"Er, English, I suppose."

"What was your last mark?" he wanted to know.

Suddenly my brain just froze. "My last mark was ..." I couldn't remember anything. "I've forgotten," I whispered.

"Forgotten?" he roared. He sounded amazed.

"You got B+, didn't you?" prompted Callum.

"Yes, that's right, I got C+. I mean B+." Grace's dad was looking at me so hard, I was getting muddled up.

"And how long do you spend on your homework each night, Ruby?"

"Oh, about an hour," I said. I didn't really know.

"An hour!" he said in shocked tones.

"Well, sometimes a bit more," I muttered.

"In my day we had three hours' homework every night," he said. "I'm always writing letters to the school about how Grace doesn't have enough homework."

"Yes, you are," said Grace, who'd just come back in with another tray of food.

Her dad got up.

"Could we have the television on now?" Grace asked him.

Her dad gave a long sigh. "You young people spend far too much time stuck in front of TVs and computer screens." And then, to my great surprise, he dug a remote out of his pocket.

He switched the television on and flicked around until he came to a programme about elephants. "Wildlife programmes are about the only thing worth watching these days. And we want to protect Grace from all the rubbish on our TV screens. She gets cross with us sometimes. But she knows we're acting in her best interests." Then he put the remote back in his pocket and marched out.

"Did you see that? He's taken the remote," cried Callum, in a shocked voice.

"They want to know exactly what I'm watching," explained Grace. "Sometimes I'll be looking at a comedy or something ... and Dad will come in and switch over to the news."

Callum said, "I can't believe your dad could take away the remote from you ... that's beyond embarrassing. That's just cruel."

Then he smiled at me. "You really shocked him when you said you only did one hour's homework!"

I laughed. "The way he looked at me then ... he's scarier than our headmaster."

"Oh, much scarier," said Grace with a grin. "So how many points do I score now?"

"Your mum scored four for making us put our bags away. And your dad easily won another four points for all those boring questions."

"And five more points for taking away the remote," I said, "and another five for making us watch a programme on elephants."

The door opened. Grace's dad came in again. "You can learn some interesting facts from those wildlife programmes, can't you, Ruby?"

"Oh, yes," I agreed.

"So what have you found out?" he asked.

"I've found out ... " I began, and once again my brain froze up. "Well, elephants are very big, aren't they?"

Grace's dad grunted and left.

"Your dad thinks I'm a total idiot, doesn't he?" I said.

Grace laughed and agreed that he did.

When we went to get our bags, Grace's mum was reading something in the hallway. She jumped when she saw us. Then I saw why. She was looking through my English exercise book. "Hope you don't mind me having a peek, Ruby," she said.

"No, that's all right," I mumbled.

"It's just you get higher marks in English than Grace. I wanted to see why." She went on, "I think, Ruby, you get more marks because your work is so neat."

I nodded. Why was Grace's mum so interested? I was amazed.

Afterwards Callum said, "That's so sad. Haven't parents got anything better to do than that? She's made a right show of herself." He grinned. "This has been a high-scoring evening all right. I don't know if Ruby's parents can beat Grace's mum and dad."

Chapter 5
My Mad Parents

When I told my parents I'd invited Grace and Callum round, they got so excited. "We were worried because you never wanted any friends round to your home," said Mum.

Then Dad said, "And don't you worry, we'll make your friends' visit really special."

On any other day those words would have terrified me. But this time my parents were going to help me win a prize. Even if Grace's parents had done well, no way could anyone be more embarrassing than my mum and dad.

It was a very warm spring day, so Mum decided we'd eat outside. She and Dad were busy setting up the picnic table in the garden when the doorbell rang.

"You go and let your friends in, Tiddles," said Mum to me with a little smile.

I opened the door to Grace and Callum.

"Where are they?" asked Callum at once.

"In the garden," I replied. "We're eating out there later." I took them into the sitting room and for the first few minutes my parents didn't turn up.

"No points scored so far," murmured Callum.

Then suddenly the door burst open – and there were my parents. What was wrong?

They were both looking serious. "Someone," Dad said grimly, "has not wiped their feet."

Grace and Callum both shifted about.

"So I must ask you, please, to show us the bottoms of your feet. Come on."

Looking very shocked, Grace and Callum both lifted up their shoes. I knew what was coming next. But they were totally fooled. Grace looked dead worried.

All at once, Mum and Dad fell about laughing. "Oh, your faces," cried Dad.

"Sorry, love," said Mum to Grace. "We were just having a little joke with you. I can promise you, you'll never, ever have to do that again. We just have one rule in this house ..." And then they both chanted, "We want you to chill! Will you do that?"

"Yes," muttered Callum.

"Can't hear you," cried Dad.

"Yes!" shouted Callum

"That's better!" said Dad. "Now just relax and have fun ... and don't mind us, because we're mad."

Mum smiled at Callum. "I bet you've never met parents like us before."

"No," he replied. "I really haven't."

Mum winked at Grace. She jumped in surprise. "Want to see a picture of Tiddles falling in a puddle?" asked Mum. And soon my awful baby photographs were passed round. Mum had about a million of those.

Callum whispered to me, "You're scoring points now, that's for sure."

Then we went outside. It was a great tea. Mum and Dad had laid on some good food, I'll give them that. And there was loads to eat.

But, of course, then Dad started to tell some more terrible jokes. "What's short and green and goes camping?" he cried. "A boy sprout!"

Mum suddenly turned to Grace and said, "Come on now, tell us all the goss ... have you got over your broken heart yet?"

Grace turned as red as a beetroot.

"That's worth another five points, definitely," hissed Callum. But he added, "Your parents are so terrible, but I like them. At least they're fun, not like poor Grace's dad. That's why her mum and dad are still winning – but only by a few points."

But something truly horrible was about to follow.

Chapter 6
Really Scary News

Dad bounded over to us. "I'm going to ask you now to step back inside." He grinned. "We have a little treat for you all."

Then he rushed off and Grace whispered, "Do you know what's happening next?"

"It could be anything," I replied.

In the sitting room Dad was waiting for us with a guitar. "I shall ask this lovely lady to tell you what's going on," he said, and he smiled at Mum as she entered the room.

"My partner here," said Mum, "feels so strongly about this wonderful planet, he's written a song called *Keep Our Planet Clean*."

"Oh, nice," said Callum, trying not to giggle. "Your parents," he said to me, "they're just wild."

I did, right then, feel an odd sort of pride in their madness.

Dad began strumming away on the guitar. He wasn't exactly bad. He wasn't exactly good. But he was OK until Mum started singing.

Years ago Mum was in a couple of adverts. She still goes on about it now. And she calls herself a part-time actress and singer. I'd heard her hum a few notes before, but it was only now I knew what a truly awful voice she had. Her singing was more like howling – the kind of sound a cat makes in the middle of the night.

"Come on, do your bit," she shrieked. "Save the planet! That means you ..." and she started pointing at us, "Yes, you and you and you." Callum was shaking with silent laughter now as Mum's voice rose even higher. "Show you care. Make a dare. Save the planet!" Then she started pointing again. "Yes, you and you and you."

Grace took off her glasses and put them on again with a shocked look on her face, as if she couldn't believe this was still going on. Callum stuffed a cushion in front of his mouth.

Suddenly my mum's voice fell away again. "The planet," she gasped. "Let's save it." Then her head fell forward as if her batteries had just run out. At the same time Dad had stopped playing the guitar. And I suddenly saw – to my total horror – that tears were running down his face.

He came forward and after a massive sniff he said, "That's all our own work." He bowed and Mum finally looked up and bowed too. Then they stood there holding hands – while we all clapped and smiled, until Dad said, "Glad you like that song, because we're singing it in your assembly on Friday."

My whole body went cold. "What?" I gasped.

"Yes, we spoke to your headmaster, Tiddles. He's doing an assembly on saving the planet. He thought it would be super to start with our song."

"Well, music can say so much more than words, can't it?" said Mum.

I couldn't reply. I just let out a very loud burp of horror.

Dad grinned. "Someone enjoyed their meal!" he said.

And then off they went to make some tea. As they left I heard Dad saying to Mum, "You brought out all the feeling in my song. Thank you so much."

I gave another big burp – the shock was making me feel as if I'd drunk twelve cans of fizzy drink all at once. Then I said, "Once they sing that song I'll have to leave my school and go somewhere else. I'll never live that down. I'll be a joke forever, won't I?"

"Well, you might be able to come back in about six months," said Grace with a kind smile.

"No, they've got to be stopped," cried Callum. "They must never sing that song in assembly."

"But how will I stop them?" I asked.

"Just tell them they stink," Callum said.

"They won't believe me," I said sadly. "They're in a dream, both of them."

Then Mum and Dad breezed back in. You could see they had no idea that they were about to totally ruin my life. Callum said to them, "Singing in assembly is really scary. Why don't you just sing it to a few friends first?"

I waited. I hoped they'd take Callum's advice, but Mum said, "Don't worry, we want to make all the pupils think."

"You'll do that all right," I murmured to myself. "They'll think you're a pair of idiots." Then I closed my eyes – and burped for a third time.

What was I to do?

Chapter 7
The Winner

How to stop Ruby's life ending after assembly on Friday.

1) Hide her dad's guitar.

2) Hide her parents' alarm clock.

3) Let all the tyres down on her dad's car.

4) Pretend Ruby has got a weird and terrible disease.

5) Pretend the school has burned down.

6) Write a letter to her parents from the headmaster, saying all assemblies have been cancelled because the ceiling in the school hall has fallen down.

Guess which suggestion we picked? Yes, that's right – Number 6. The others were just too risky – or mad. But Number 6 could work. Callum is brilliant at faking signatures. My parents would really think the letter had come from the head.

But to make sure, the letter had to be on proper school paper. This was kept in Miss Green's office. At break time, when she was getting her coffee in the staff room, Callum could slip in and take some notepaper. It would be easy.

There was just one problem with this plan. Miss Green never left to get any coffee. Instead, she stayed in her office all during break.

46

Callum, Grace and I peered in at Miss Green working away in her office. "Everyone else is going in and out and having chats, but not her," groaned Callum.

"Couldn't we just write the letter on ordinary paper?" said Grace.

"We could," said Callum, "but having the letter written on proper school paper adds that extra touch. And it's important that Ruby's parents believe it."

"Very important," I agreed. Then I had an idea. Why didn't I pretend to faint right outside Miss Green's office? She'd dash out and comfort me, and Callum could nip in and grab the notepaper.

"Do you think you can do that?" said Grace. She was looking worried again. "You won't get the giggles – like you sometimes do?"

"No, this is too important," I said.

I stood right in front of Miss Green's office. Then I let out a cry of pain. Miss Green didn't even look up. So then I gave a great yell of torment, which sounded very much like Mum's singing. Miss Green heard that all right. She jumped up and charged out of her office and over to me.

At once I started swaying about. Grace said afterwards I looked as if I was dancing – not about to faint. But Miss Green was really upset about me.

"Whatever's the matter?" she cried. She was a small, thin woman who wore those glasses which hang on a chain round your neck.

"I was just standing here," I gasped, "when I got this awful pain."

"Where?" she demanded.

"Well, the pain started in my head," I said, with a deep sigh, "but now it's down my arms as well, and all across my back." Then, worrying I was over-doing it a bit, I added, "But my legs are still OK."

"I'll call the nurse for you," she said. "Come and sit down in my office."

I could see Callum was still in her office, madly hunting for the school notepaper. I said, "Can I just stand here a bit longer? I can't breathe properly." I started taking great gulps of air.

Miss Green watched me. She looked even more alarmed. "I really think the nurse should have a look at you at once … " she said.

Then I saw Callum creep out of the office. "Got it," he mouthed at me.

"Do you know what?" I said to Miss Green. "Suddenly I feel much better."

"What!" she spluttered.

"Yeah, all that pain has suddenly vanished." Then the bell went. "You've been a great help," I cried. "Bye!" I sped away before Miss Green could stop me.

At lunchtime the three of us charged over to Callum's house to write the fake letter.

Dear Mr and Mrs Adams

I hope you are both enjoying good health.

Sad news, I'm afraid - part of the ceiling in the school hall has fallen down. It happened right out of the blue as well. Luckily no one was hurt, except for the caretaker. He's got bruises everywhere but is still smiling.

Unfortunately, we now have nowhere to hold assemblies, so they've all been cancelled - probably for years.

I remain your humble headmaster.

And then came the very best part of the letter ... the autograph. Callum copied the headmaster's signature brilliantly. Grace and I (and, to be honest, Callum as well) kept admiring it.

G. Warrington

Giles Warrington

Your Headmaster

"Now that autograph would fool anyone," I said. Callum nodded proudly.

Back at school I went to see Miss Green again. "How are you feeling?" she asked. She sounded nervous.

"Never better," I said. "But could you tell the headmaster that my parents won't be able to sing at the assembly tomorrow – they've both lost their voices."

"Oh, dear," cried Miss Green.

"Yes, they just rang up ... I mean, they sent me a text message."

"Have they got sore throats?" asked Miss Green.

"Yes, that's exactly what they've got," I agreed. "Still, it'll be nice and quiet at home tonight, won't it?"

I didn't go round to Callum's house after school. "I want to deliver this letter to my parents right away," I said.

"Well, just before you dash off," said Callum, "I'd like to award you this." Then he handed me a little certificate, on which he'd written,

RUBY, YOU DEFINITELY HAVE

THE MOST EMBARRASSING PARENTS EVER.

Congratulations for putting up with them.

"So I won," I smiled.

"In the end, you walked it," he replied. "Thanks to their singing."

I was humming a little to myself as I arrived home. Suddenly I felt everything was going to work out. Then I got a shock. Mum and Dad were both waiting for me. "We're just popping in to your school for a few minutes. We want to get a look at the hall."

"So we can pick up the vibes for tomorrow," grinned Dad. "All the top singers like to do that."

I jumped in shock. "Sorry, Dad," I cried. "All assemblies have been cancelled."

"You're joking!" cried Dad.

"Why?" asked Mum.

They both looked so upset I almost felt sorry for them. "I've got a letter all about it from the headmaster," I said.

I opened my bag – and guess what – I couldn't find that letter anywhere. Where had I put it? I threw everything out, while Mum and Dad stood watching me.

"I know it's here somewhere," I cried. I was panicking when at last I saw it. I picked the letter up and, a bit out of breath, I handed it to my mum.

"It's all explained in there," I said.

And then something truly awful happened.

I noticed Dad looking down at something. My heart started to race madly. But it was too late to do anything. Dad had already picked up the certificate which said

RUBY, YOU DEFINITELY HAVE

THE MOST EMBARRASSING PARENTS EVER.

He looked very puzzled and confused. "Whatever is this, Ruby?" he asked.

"Oh, that," I laughed. "That is ..." What could I tell him? I struggled to think of something.

Anything.

And then I saw Mum pick up the score sheet, which Callum had also given me to go with the certificate.

That's when I knew I was in big trouble.

Chapter 8

What Parents Must Never Do

The next hour was just awful.

I decided I wouldn't try and make something up. I was in too much of a mess. No, I'd tell my mum and dad the truth. They'd been voted the most embarrassing parents ever. I thought they'd laugh about it. But for once they didn't even smile. In fact, I thought Dad was going to fall down on the carpet with shock.

"But who voted?" asked Mum.

I explained what had happened.

"And we won?" whispered Mum.

"By how many votes?" asked Dad.

"By a few," I said softly.

"But what's embarrassing about us?" Dad went on. "We're so hip and friendly ..."

"A little bit too friendly, sometimes," I said. "And you do mad things, like ... singing in assembly."

"And what's wrong with that?" cried Mum. "We're singing to save the environment, Tiddles."

"Parents must never, ever sing," I said firmly. "That's one of the most shameful things you can ever do. Another is giving their children really embarrassing nicknames – like Tiddles."

"You don't like us calling you Tiddles?" gasped Mum, in a really shocked voice.

"I totally hate it," I said.

There was a stunned silence for a moment. Then Dad asked, "What other things shouldn't parents do?"

"Parents must never dance, laugh loudly, talk loudly, or wear clothes that are too young for them." I waited for a moment. "Or tell bad jokes."

Dad suddenly looked away. He couldn't say a word at first. Then he muttered softly, "Well, I think my jokes are funny."

"That letter you gave us wasn't really from the headmaster, was it?" said Mum.

"No," I admitted. "It was, in fact, a very clever fake. I know I shouldn't have done it but I got so panicky. I mean, if you had sung in assembly tomorrow, I'd have had to leave my school, and maybe never, ever come back."

58

Mum and Dad both sank down on the couch. They looked like two burst balloons. "We thought we were the best parents," said Dad. "You know how gloomy your grandad is? I thought I'd be the total opposite – always cheerful and happy. But instead – we're the most embarrassing parents ever. I just can't believe it."

"It's like a bad dream," agreed Mum.

Then Dad said, "So really, you don't want your parents to have any fun?" He sounded a bit cross.

"Yes, I do!" I cried. "But in secret, and never, ever in public. And when you meet my friends just be careful not to mention modern bands, or old ones either. And don't ask them any questions – apart from 'How are you?' That's OK to ask. But otherwise, say nothing."

"You know the really amazing thing," said Mum. "I thought we were more like your friends than parents. I thought you told us everything."

"No teenager tells their parents everything," I said.

"Well, don't worry," said Mum. "We had a very important message for everyone but we shan't sing in assembly tomorrow."

"Thank you," I whispered. Then I added, "When you're on your own you can still sing."

"You're very kind," said Mum.

For the rest of the evening Mum and Dad hardly spoke. The silence wasn't as good as you'd think. It felt kind of spooky, somehow. And Mum and Dad both seemed fed up, and so lost.

As I was going to bed Mum said. "Don't forget this," and handed me my certificate.

She looked so hurt, I cried, "Shall I rip it up?"

"Oh no," said Mum at once. "You won that for putting up with us. It's yours. Well done! You must hang it up on your wall, if you like."

"I couldn't do that," I cried.

And upstairs I just threw it into the bottom of a drawer.

Next day at school I told Callum and Grace what had happened.

"You should have taken your bag and looked through it in your bedroom, not right in front of your parents," said Callum.

"I know," I agreed. "It's just, I panicked."

Grace said, "Still, at least you haven't got them singing in assembly ... that's something."

"Oh, yes," I agreed. "It's just they keep looking at me with such hurt, sad eyes."

I really did not want to go home for the weekend. This was going to be so awful. But when Mum saw me she was smiling – a little. "Hello, dear, have a nice day?" she said.

When Dad came in, he said. "Ruby, we learnt a lot yesterday. And now we'd like you to help us. Will you do that?"

"Yes," I agreed. What were they thinking?

"Well, our idea," said Mum, "might sound a little odd, but I think it will be good for everyone."

I listened to their idea. This, I hadn't expected.

Chapter 9
A Shocking Discovery

Later that day I rang up Callum.

"Would you like to come round my house for your tea tomorrow afternoon?" I added, "I should warn you, my parents asked for you to come round."

"But why would they do that?" Callum asked.

"I'm not sure," I answered.

"They know I was the judge in the embarrassing parents competition ... so now they're planning to get their revenge on me," he said.

"Maybe, I just don't know ... but they say they've learnt their lesson and want to show me how well they can behave."

"Hmm." Callum thought about it. After a bit he said, "Of course I'll come round. I can't wait to see what your parents'll do now."

Next afternoon my mum and dad hardly said a word. I sensed something was going on. But I didn't know what it could be. And when the doorbell rang they didn't rush to answer it, as they did every time. Instead, Dad just said, "We'll leave you to answer that, Ruby," and trooped upstairs with Mum following.

I opened the door to Callum. He started looking round for my mum and dad.

"They've both marched upstairs," I said. Then I called out, "Mum, Dad, Callum's here."

There was no answer.

We went into the sitting room. I could hear my parents moving about upstairs, but then that stopped and there was silence.

"This is very weird," hissed Callum. "Are they just sitting upstairs sulking? Or perhaps they're showing us they can leave us alone."

Then we heard footsteps coming down the stairs.

"Here we go," said Callum.

We waited. We were both feeling nervous.

The door to the sitting room opened very slowly. And I let out a shocked gasp. Mum was standing there. And she was wearing the longest black dress I'd ever seen. It went right down to her ankles. She also had a funny little black shawl on her head. She didn't seem anything like my mum. Even her face looked different. She was so serious.

"Good afternoon," she said, and bowed her head a little.

"Hello Mrs Adams," said Callum.

"Greetings, young sir," Mum said, and bowed her head again.

I laughed in astonishment. "Why are you talking like that?"

But not a flicker of a smile crossed Mum's face. Instead, she asked softly, "Would either of you like to have some light refreshment?"

Callum was looking at her in total amazement. His mouth was wide open. But I decided to play along. "Yes, please, we'll have a pot of tea and some of your best cakes."

"It will be done at once," replied Mum, and she bowed again. Then she left and shut the door very slowly behind her.

As soon as she'd gone, Callum cried out. "That *was* your mum, wasn't it?" Then he muttered, "Ssh," as the door opened again. This time it was my dad who stood there, dressed in a black suit. He bowed low, then walked slowly over to the table, with a tray of cakes.

"The tea is to follow, young lady, and young sir," he said.

"Dad, what is all this?" I asked.

Dad ignored my question. He put the cakes on the table. The look on his face was so grave he'd have made Count Dracula look cheerful.

Then Mum came back in with a large pot of tea. She insisted on pouring out the tea and giving us both milk and sugar. Mum and Dad then stood in front of the doorway. "Is there anything else you require?" asked Mum.

"Just for you two to stop acting so silly," I said.

"Oh, we'll never act silly again," replied Dad in a low voice. "You won't ever catch us laughing, singing, talking loudly or telling bad jokes." Dad gave a little gulp here. "And that's a promise." Then, with a final bow the two of them left.

As soon as they'd gone Callum was laughing, fit to burst. He said, "I could never imagine my dad and step-mum acting like that."

"You're lucky," I replied.

"Not really," he said. "Sometimes I think the real family is my dad, my step-mum and their two kids. I'm just an add-on, the lodger. And the reason they've given me my own room downstairs is just so I don't bother them."

"Oh, that's not true," I cried.

"It's a bit true," he replied. "They give me too much freedom – as if I'm not really anything to do with them. I don't have many laughs with my family either ... sometimes I even wish they were a bit more embarrassing."

I'd never heard Callum say any of this before. He suddenly started laughing again. "Your mum and dad," he said. "They're just wild."

"Yes they are," I agreed. And I suddenly felt proud of them.

Mum and Dad came in and cleared away, in their solemn way. And when Callum asked Dad how he was feeling, he replied. "Very well, young sir ... and thank you so much for your interest."

When Callum left, Mum handed him his coat with a final bow. "I trust you enjoyed your visit, young sir," she said.

"It's something I shall never forget," he replied. Then he winked at me.

After he'd gone I turned round and faced my parents. I was half-annoyed, half-laughing. "What on earth was that all about?" I had to know.

"Well, it's what you wanted, isn't it?" cried Mum. Her eyes lit up as she went on. "You didn't want parents who sang, laughed or chatted with your friends. No, you wanted parents who wore drab clothes, didn't say anything and just handed round food and drinks ... you wanted us to act like servants in Victorian times, in fact."

"No!" I cried.

"Oh, yes, you did," said Mum. "So we thought we'd show you what life would be like if we did that."

I suddenly saw something. Un-embarrassing parents can be really dull and dreary. My mum and dad were fun – and a good laugh. And I'd miss that.

That came as a shock to me. But I knew it was true. I'd been a little mean to Mum and Dad, hadn't I? I felt ashamed now. I gave them a big smile and said, "You know what? I like my parents being a bit embarrassing."

Mum smiled back at me.

"Well, we promise we'll never call you Tiddles in front of your friends. And there'll be no singing in assembly. Ever!"

"Thank you very much," I said.

"The only thing is," said Dad, "we've practised that song so many times. We made it much better too and we'd love someone to hear it." He and Mum started looking at me with hopeful faces.

"All right," I said. "You can play your song for me."

Dad ran upstairs to get his guitar. Then Mum and Dad, still in their servants' uniforms, began to sing me their song about saving the planet once more. And of course, it was awful. The funny thing is, though, it didn't seem quite so awful as before. And I could say, "It's definitely better than it was." That was the truth.

How Mum and Dad's eyes sparkled then! Well, you've got to encourage your parents now and again, haven't you?

In fact, my dad got so excited he started telling jokes again.

"What's round, white and giggles?" he cried. "A tickled onion!"

And do you know what – I even laughed.

Barrington Stoke would like to thank all its readers for commenting on the manuscript before publication and in particular:

Heather Boyd

Harriet Darby

Claire Vardy

Become a Consultant!

Would you like to give us feedback on our titles before they are published? Contact us at the email address below – we'd love to hear from you!

info@barringtonstoke.co.uk
www.barringtonstoke.co.uk

Also by the same author ...

The Best Holiday Ever!

by Pete Johnson

Annette, Sarah and Katie are off on their first ever holiday WITHOUT their parents ... and they can't wait!

Will they meet the boys of their dreams and make this a holiday to remember? Or will World War Three break out between Katie and Annette?

WITHDRAWN

You can order *The Best Holiday Ever!* directly from our website at **www.barringtonstoke.co.uk**